Lions are top hunters. They eat buffalo, deer, gazelle, impala, warthog, wildebeest and zebra.

There are about 25,000 lions left in the wild. Most live in Africa, with a small group living in a protected area in India.

tail

Lion

claws

mane

Lions live in groups called prides. There are about 15 lions in each pride. Lions may sleep for up to 20 hours a day.

Male lions have a thick mane of hair around their heads.

The latin name for the lion is *Panthera leo*

All lion cubs are born with blue eyes, which change to brown when they are about 3 months old.

Female lions are usually the hunters in the pride. The males protect the territory where they live.

The growing human population means that much of the lions' habitat is being converted into settlements and agriculture. This means there is less prey for the lions to hunt.

The roar of an adult male can be heard up to 5 miles away.

A big male lion can weigh up to 440lbs. Females are usually lighter, weighing around 286lbs.

For Sienna and Monet
Be more Lion! xx

First published in 2021 by Child's Play (International) Ltd
Ashworth Road, Bridgemead, Swindon SN5 7YD, UK

First published in USA in 2021 by Child's Play Inc
250 Minot Avenue, Auburn, Maine 04210

Distributed in Australia by Child's Play Australia Pty Ltd
Unit 10/20 Narabang Way, Belrose, Sydney, NSW 2085

ISBN 978-1-78628-470-9
SJ200320CPL04204709

Printed in Shenzhen, China

1 3 5 7 9 10 8 6 4 2

A catalogue record of this book
is available from the British Library

www.childs-play.com

Bea by the Sea

Jo Byatt

Bea loved lions.
No one knew more about lions than Bea!

Bea thought about lions all day long.

What do they eat for breakfast?

Would lions like a bubbly bath?

Do lions visit the dentist?

How many teeth do they have?

How fast can lions run?

One day Mom said,
"It's a lovely morning.
Let's go to the beach!"

"Do we have to?" asked Bea. "Can't we just stay and play here?"

Bea didn't like sand at all.
It was too gritty, too sticky,
and too scratchy, especially
when it got between her toes.

Bea put her boots on,
and packed her lion stuff.

"I'll pretend I'm a lion,"
she thought.
"They aren't afraid
of anything!"

Bea was a bit wobbly,
but she managed
to hop from rock
to rock without
touching any sand.

"Wow!" exclaimed Mom. "Look at those sand sculptures! They're amazing!"

But Bea was far too busy not touching the sand.

All of a sudden, she tripped over
something and fell flat on her face.

In the sand!

Bea frantically
brushed the sand
off her face.

"Hello!
I'm Sand Lion,"
boomed
a loud voice.
"Who are you?"

"I'm Bea," she replied.
"I don't like sand,
and I'm covered in it!
And where's my boot?"

"You're missing out,"
replied Sand Lion.
"Come and see!"

"Making footprints in
the sand is much better
with your boots off!"
explained Sand Lion.

"Ooh!" Bea squealed.
"It feels so scratchy!"

Sand Lion thought she was doing really well.

They listened to the sound of the sea.

"It's just like your roar!" giggled Bea.

They built a giant sandcastle.

They made a big sand angel. And a little sand angel.

Until Bea was covered in sand!

"I guess sand isn't so bad," said Bea.
"But I think I'll wash it off my hands now."
She looked up. "What's the matter, Sand Lion?"

All About Lions

"I really don't like water," he shivered.

"It's okay when you get used to it," said Bea.
"Let's try jumping over these little waves."

Bea thought Sand Lion was doing really well.

At the end of the day, it was time to go home.

"The tide's coming in!"
Mom shouted. "Let's go, Bea!"

"See you tomorrow,
Sand Lion!" smiled Bea.
"We'll have such fun!"

The next morning, Bea couldn't
wait to get to the beach.

"Slow down!" laughed Mom.
"I thought you didn't like sand?"

But when they arrived there was
nothing left of the sand sculptures.
The sandcastle had gone.

And Sand Lion
had disappeared, too!

Bea felt sad. She sat down on the sand
and looked out to sea. The roar of the waves
reminded her of Sand Lion's voice.

She remembered all the fun they'd had...

...and she knew just what to do.

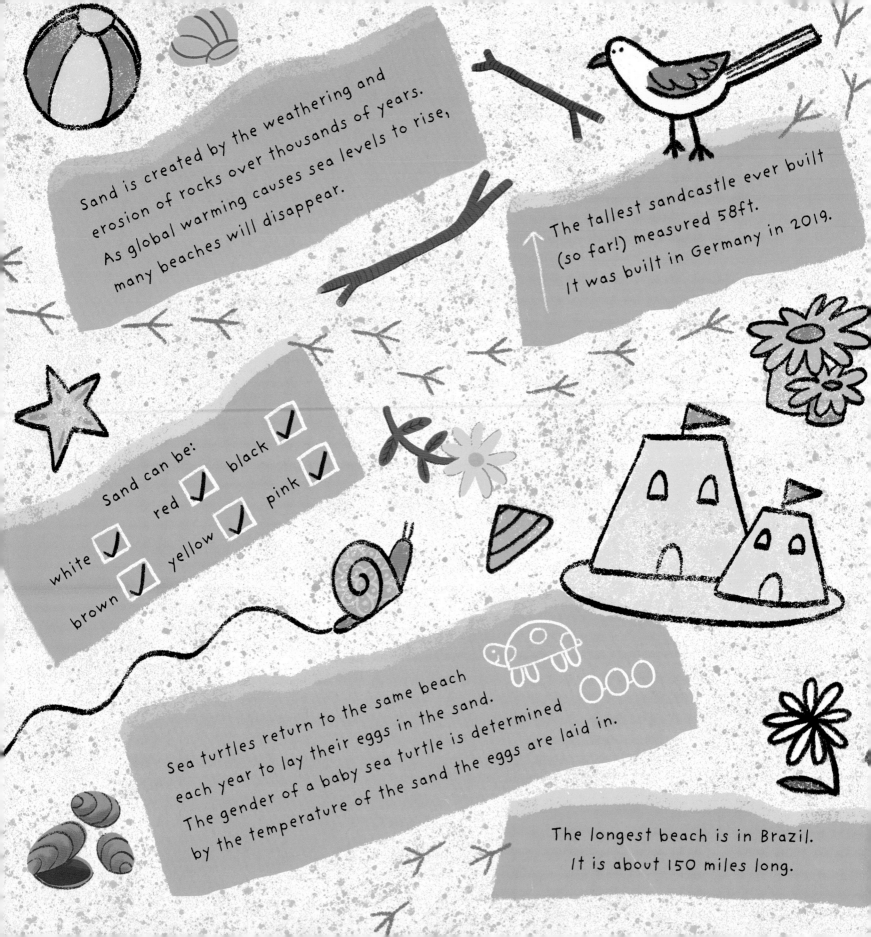

Sand is created by the weathering and erosion of rocks over thousands of years. As global warming causes sea levels to rise, many beaches will disappear.

The tallest sandcastle ever built (so far!) measured 58ft. It was built in Germany in 2019.

Sand can be:
- white ✓
- red ✓
- black ✓
- brown ✓
- yellow ✓
- pink ✓

Sea turtles return to the same beach each year to lay their eggs in the sand. The gender of a baby sea turtle is determined by the temperature of the sand the eggs are laid in.

The longest beach is in Brazil. It is about 150 miles long.

Sand is used to make glass, concrete, and bricks.

I ♥ sand

A dune is a mound of sand formed by the wind. Sand gets trapped and the dunes grow bigger and bigger.

Desert sand cannot be used in the building industry as it is too smooth and difficult to stick together.

A person who collects sand for a hobby is called an arenophile.

Sand is made of tiny particles of rock, minerals, shellfish, and coral.

Driftwood and seaweed washed ashore creates shelter and a rich food source for creatures on the beach. A perfect habitat for crabs, starfish, snails and many others.